There are fourteen hidden treasures inside of this book. Can you find them?

To Shawn, Reilly, Morgan, Hadley, and Colin.
You are love and you are loved! -Suzanne

To Brandon, Harlow, Maddax, and Zeke.
May you always know yourself as love. -Ashley

Generation Mindful, LLC
20 South Sarah Street
St. Louis, Missouri 63108

ISBN 9780578594477
Printed in China
Design by Courtney Tharpe
www.GenMindful.com

HEART'S TREASURE HUNT

ASHLEY PATEK
SUZANNE TUCKER

Illustrations by: Roxana Farcas

Is **LOVE** a treasure
we touch and we hold?

Is LOVE
something
we see?

Or a word
that we're told?

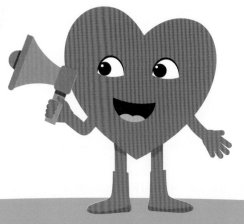

Is LOVE in
my happy?

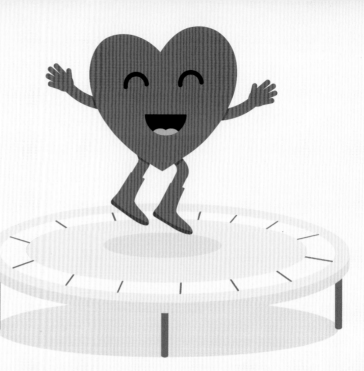

Is LOVE in my sad?

4

Is LOVE in my body when I'm calm?

When I'm mad?

Does LOVE have a shape?
Does LOVE have a color?

Is LOVE
always there?

We are here
to DISC♥VER!

Listening and looking

How do we know?

Searching high, high, high, high.

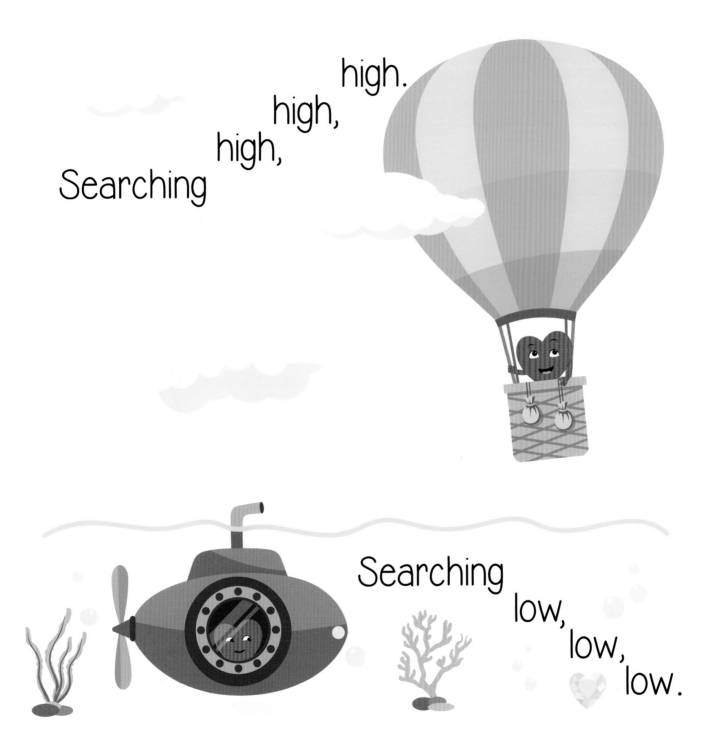

Searching low, low, low.

FOLLOW ME friends,
inside of this book.

One page at a time,
let's have a look!

HOORAY!

Our love treasure hunt begins!

Brave **RED BEAR**,
in your safe cave of love...

Is love cozy like your gentle bear hug?

Can you give yourself **a big** Red Bear **hug?**

Silly **ORANGE FOX**, with your disco dance...
Can love be felt in your playful love prance?

Can you **dance** like **silly** Orange Fox?

15

In the tall grass,
YELLOW LION snores.

Is love hiding behind your big, fierce roar?

GREEN HUMMINGBIRD
flutters high with love.

Do you feel
the love message
from above?

Can you
**flap your
wings** like
Green
Hummingbird?

BLUE DOLPHIN swims in the blue lagoon.
Do you hear the sweet and peaceful love tune?

Can you **squeak** like Blue Dolphin?

INDIGO OWL hoots loud, "Hoo, hoo, hoo."
Is love a voice that lives inside of you?

Can you **hoot** like Indigo Owl?

23

VIOLET ELEPHANT,
big and true.

Does love and forgiveness help me grow too?

Can you reach **up high** like Violet Elephant's long trunk?

Love must be hiding
inside of this book.

Behind the last page,
let's have a look!

YOU ARE LOVE
YES, IT'S TRUE
LOVE, LOVE, LOVE,
LOVE IS YOU!

LETTER TO THE READER:

Hello and thank you for spreading the Generation Mindful love! Together we can teach children it is SAFE to feel, and turn "stop crying" into "I'm listening" for an entire generation. In this book, Heart is on a journey to discover not only what love is, but where it lives. Children are on a similar journey, studying the world around them and drawing conclusions about who they are and whether or not they are safe. At Generation Mindful, we want EVERY child to have a mirror held up to them that reflects back the love that they are. ***Because truly, we are love and we are enough, today, right now, just the way we are...even as we learn and grow.***

Love lives inside each and every one of us. This is the treasure we discover at the end of this book. It's easy for kids to see emotions as either good or bad, right or wrong, but Heart and our PeaceMakers animal friends help children remember the love they are ALL the time. Happy, sad, calm, fearful or mad, our emotions are here to teach us about ourselves and the world around us. You are love, yes it's true. Love, love, love, love is YOU.

Suzanne

To help you bring this book to life, here are some playful and engaging tips:

PUT ON YOUR LISTENING EARS

As you read this book aloud to children, practice pausing between each page. Use your body language to connect with children - a smile, a silly dance, a reassuring pat, or your loving eye contact alone, minus words. Sometimes our hugs speak louder than our words. As an adult, reading this book to children is a wonderful opportunity for us to move into our listening bodies.

ENGAGE THE SENSES

Emotions are felt within our feeling bodies and so in the story, children are invited playfully to practice tuning into their many senses. What do they see, hear, feel? Engaging the world through the senses is a wonderful way to sharpen one's ability to recognize, understand, label and express emotions.

FOLLOW YOUR CHILD'S LEAD

This book is full of natural prompts to get children thinking, talking, moving and playing. Read it through a few times before making suggestions and see what playful ideas your child naturally comes up with.

MAKE IT A RITUAL

Children love structure. Rituals are predictable and therefore can more easily put the human brain at ease and help it to feel safe. As you read this book again and again, notice the rituals that you and the children you share it with create together. Embrace the many daily, playful rituals you share together and make connection a habit.

LEARN THROUGH PLAY

Play is learning! Play is how the human brain was actually designed to learn, and play is the most important foundation for all social emotional learning that your child will experience in their lifetime. Open yourself up to the many playful ideas this story might spark in you and in children. Build a fort out of pillows and blankets like Red Bear's cave, have a dance party every night like silly fox, roar big roars when you feel like a lion inside, and give that feeling a name, etc. Being playful as you read this story and teach children about their emotions helps to make it safe for kids to feel all their many feelings.

ABOUT ASHLEY & SUZANNE

Ashley is an occupational therapist, holistic lifestyle coach, and chief storyteller with Generation Mindful. Her tribe consists of her supportive husband, Brandon and her three blessings, Harlow, Maddax, and Zeke. She is called to nature, moves with her heart, enjoys connecting with others, writing, and all things family. Just an education seekin', acai bowl lovin', Sunday brunch-havin', free-spirited mama!

Suzanne is a physical therapist, parent educator, mom of four, and the founder of Generation Mindful. Her bliss is inspiring connection. She loves yoga, hiking, being married to a man who likes to cook, the ocean, and family vacations. If she had one superpower, it would be to help all people feel a deep sense of peace and belonging, no matter the circumstances of their lives.

Visit **GENMINDFUL.COM** for more

HEART'S TREASURE HUNT

learning inspirations, lesson plans, printables, and more.

"A beautiful and loving adventure for kids, Heart's Treasure invites the young reader to find the love in everyday experiences in life. Filled with inspiring images and reminders of the preciousness of our connections with each other and nature, this book will be treasured by kids, young and old!"

-Daniel J. Siegel, New York Times bestselling author, *Aware, Mind*, and co-author, *Parenting from the Inside Out* and *The Power of Showing Up*

"What does this world need more of? Love! In this sweet, playful picture book, the masterminds behind Generation Mindful share an important message for children and adults alike. Sometimes the most profound messages come in the simplest of books."

-Audrey Monke, mom, camp director, and author of *Happy Campers*

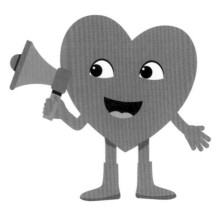